The Wonderful World of Chocolate

A.P. Hernández

Translated by Karina Jimenez

"The Wonderful World of Chocolate: Welcome to SugarVille!"

Written By A.P. Hernández

Copyright © 2019 A.P. Hernández

Translated by Karina Jimenez

About the author:

Antonio Pérez Hernández is a Primary Education teacher (specializing in Musical, Auditory and Language Education and Therapeutic Teaching). A pedagogue, he has a Master's in Educational Research and Innovation, and a Doctorate for which he was awarded *cum laude* for his Doctoral Thesis "Evaluation of Competence in Linguistic Communication Through Stories in Primary Education."

He came second in the Nemira Prize for Literary Creation and was a finalist in the Dagón International Fantasy and Horror Novel Competition.

He has published more than fifty books, which have been translated into seven languages: Dutch, English, French, German, Greek, Italian and Portuguese.

He currently combines teaching and writing.

Website: www.aphernandez.com

Chapter 1

A sweet start

Daniel likes chocolate. Actually, he loves chocolate! Every chocolate is welcome: black chocolate, white chocolate, milk chocolate, chocolate with cereals and dried fruits, chocolate with fruit, and of course, pure chocolate.

Daniel likes chocolate so much that his favorite words start with "choco," specially: chocolate shop and chocolate milk.

Right now, Daniel is eight years old and he is already clear on what he wants to be when he grows up: a chocolatier.

Daniel wants to work in a chocolate factory and spend the whole day surrounded by such delicious treats.

Chapter 2

A magical world

But a couple of days ago, Daniel's life gave a radical turn.

It all started at his best friend Roberto's birthday party.

He celebrated his birthday at his country house and invited a bunch of friends: Noelia, Alejandro, Sara, Maria, Antonio, Nerea...

The celebration was fantastic, because Roberto has a huge pool.

They listened to music, dipped in the pool, danced, played cops and robbers and even invented a game similar to soccer, but underwater.

And just when Daniel thought he couldn't be having a better time, like straight out of heaven, came the cake.

All the children ran towards it and started singing happy birthday to Roberto.

But Daniel didn't sing.

He was paralyzed!

With his mouth wide open, he solemnly stared at the birthday cake.

It was made of chocolate, huge and best of all, shaped like a castle!

Daniel had never seen anything like it before.

The castle had five battlements (all of them also made of chocolate) and was surrounded by a moat in which you could see tiny crocodiles swimming in a river of delicious chocolate.

That night, when Daniel got home, the impressive image of the chocolate castle is still engraved in his mind.

Before falling asleep, he makes a wish:

"I wish I could live in a world of chocolate!"

Daniel looks over at Canica, his Chihuahua dog. Canica, although tiny, is more than ten years old. She has been living with his parents even before he was born

"Would you like to live in a world of chocolate?" he asks the dog.

Canica rolls into a ball on her cushion and watches him with her bright black eyes.

"A chocolate world..." says Daniel to himself, falling asleep. "Where everything is made out of sugar... A magical world..."

And with that thought, Daniel falls into a deep sleep.

Chapter 3

Wow Chihuahua!

"Wake up Daniel," says the voice. "Quick! Look at this!"

Daniel turns in bed. He's not willing to wake up just like that.

"I'm sleepy..." he says to the voice. "I want to sleep..."

Next, silence. Daniel takes advantage of this to sink his face into the plushy pillow but, just when he's about to fall asleep again, he feels a great force smack him on the back.

"Wake up, Daniel!" says the same voice, louder. "Look at this!"

Daniel jumps, startled.

And then, he sees it.

Daniel rubs his eyes.

"It can't be real," he says to himself, closing and opening his eyes hard. "It's impossible..."

Right next to him, a huge eagle is talking to him. The bird is enormous... even bigger than a horse...

And, although Daniel know it is impossible, he sees something familiar in its look.

The eagle has black, bright eyes, just like...

"Canica... Is that you?"

The eagle smiles, bowing in clear sign of courtesy.

"Yes, Daniel. I'm your faithful friend, Canica."

"But... You're a dog... A Chihuahua... How is it possible...?"

But Daniel can't finish his sentence. Just then, he realizes.

He realizes that Canica hasn't turned into a giant eagle... but some species of lion with wings and the head of a bird.

Canica steps in front of Daniel.

She has pink wings and a huge, long, feline tail. But the best thing are her head's feathers. They are a delicate and beautiful cream color.

"What have you turned into?" asks Daniel.

Suddenly, he starts relaxing. The whole thing doesn't make him nervous anymore. He's more amused than anything.

"Are you a lion or a bird?"

Daniel approaches Canica and pets her head. Just as he suspected, her feathers are extremely soft.

"I'm not a lion," Canica answers, moving her beak as if it was a mouth. "And as you can imagine, I'm not any species of bird either."

"Then...?"

"I'm a griffin," Canica's words are filled with pride.

"Wow!" Daniel has never heard that word. "How fun!"

Canica gives a few steps towards him, driving her powerful claws into the ground. She stops a couple of centimeters away. Canica is so close to Daniel, he can almost smell her breath.

She has a huge head... and smiles at him.

"Enough chit-chat, my friend," she says, winking at him. "Why don't we go take a look around?"

Chapter 4
Higher, please

Daniel hops onto Canica's back. He realizes that her back is totally different from her front. Her back is featherless and has a strong yello pelt... Just like a lion!

"Are you sure," Daniel asks, grabbing onto her head's feathers. "Sure you can handle me?"

Canica laughs.

"You hardly weight anything!" she assures him. "Just hold on tight!"

And Canica starts running. She is going so quick, Daniel feels the air slap his face. Afraid of falling, he hangs onto Canica's neck as if his life depended on it.

When Canica reaches enough speed, she unfolds her huge wings and starts flapping them. Daniel listens to the sound made on each shake:

BUUUMMMMM - BUUUMMMMM
BUUUMMMMMMM

Canica flaps her wings faster.

BUUMM- BUUMMM- BUUMM- BUUMM-
BUUMM- BUUMM

And then, a little faster:

BUMM, BUMM, BUMM, BUMM, BUMM...

And, just like that, with a simple jump, she jumps into the air.

Daniel laughs, he laughs loudly.

He's flying... Each time higher... Higher! Higher!

And he starts seeing the landscape.

He doesn't know where he is but... But... Everything is made out of sugar!

Chapter 5

An extraordinary world

That world was extraordinary.

Daniele can't find the words to describe what his eyes see. Everywhere he looks, he sees only candy of bright and cheerful colors.

After a long flight, Canica decides it's time to rest, so with a slight inclination, starts descending.

Little by little they lose height. Canica no longer flaps her wings, but only glides. Every now and then, she leans one way or the other, using the weight of her body to direct the landing

Daniel says nothing. He stays contemplating the mastery with which his faithful dog friend, not turned into a griffin, handles herself in the air.

"I'm landing there," points out Canica.

Daniel sees a clearing in the woods. It seems like a quiet place.

"Great!" he says.

Canica continues her descent and, barely 20 meters away from the ground, flaps forward, stopping her horizontal travel.

Suddenly, they stay suspended in the air, static. But it doesn't take long for gravity to appear. In the blink of an eye, Daniel sees himself descending vertically, like you would in an elevator.

But to his surprise, the fall is soft.

Canica has hollowed out here huger wings, like a parachute.

Finally, they step on solid ground.

Chapter 6

Too quiet

They find themselves in a clearing of a strange forest.

Canica lays down by the trunk of a tree and, with a relaxed gestures, starts grooming her wings.

"I'm going to explore!" he says to his friend.

Canica takes her head out of between her right wing feathers and watches him, a little worried.

"Alright... But don't go too far."

Daniel takes a path to the thick of the woods.

He doesn't have to walk long before he understands that, just as he had imagined from the air, everything surrounding him is made out of sugar.

The bushes are gummies and, instead of fruits, they have jelly beans. Daniel, unable to resist, takes a jelly bean and eats it.

"It's delicious!" he says.

It's strawberry, although there are a lot of other

flavors.

He keeps on walking and checks that the rocks in the woods are, actually, huge pieces of licorice.

Daniel checks a bit better and discovers that the dirt he's stepping on isn't actually dirt. It's actually cookie crumble.

He goes towards a zone he hasn't stepped in and burying his fingers in the dirt, takes a fistful of cookie.

He eats it and finds that is has a soft vanilla smell.

Daniel walks around for a while in the forest, but doesn't discover anything new. So he turns around and goes back to the clearing.

He follows the path of a river that, instead of water, carries liquid chocolate.

Daniel stops, makes a bowl with his hands and dips them in the river. Very carefully, he takes the liquid to his mouth and... Drinks.

"It's delicious!" he says surprised.

It's hot cocoa. It has the same taste as the one he drinks on Saturdays when his mother makes him coco to go with the churros and fritters.

Daniel returns to Canica. The griffin is nibbling an apple.

"Hey, there is fruit!" Daniel says. "Which means that not everything is made out of sugar in this world."

"You're wrong," Canica says, snapping the apple in half with a quick movement of her beak. "This apple has sugar... It's a caramel apple!"

Daniel raises his hand and takes one of the many fruits hanging from the apple tree. Just by touching it, he realizes his friend is right.

"It's covered in caramel!"

It has so much caramel, that Daniel ends up with his hands all sticky.

He'd go to the river to wash them, but that wouldn't do anything except make it worse. Daniel remembers there is no water.

So, doing his best, he wipes his hands on his pants legs.

In silence, he observes Canica devour a bunch of apples. When she's finished, they look at each other.

"This whole world... It's really quiet, don't you think?"

The griffin nods.

"Canica... Do you think we're the only living things in this planet?"

"I don't know, Daniel," she answers. "We might be... Or we might not be. So far we haven't seen anybody... Not even an animal."

It is right then when Daniel realizes.

He keeps quiet and listens to his surroundings.

Nothing.

He hears absolutely nothing.

Except for the bubbling of the hot cocoa river, the rest is silence.

No whisper of the wind, no birds chirping, none of the other sounds he was so used to on planet Earth.

Chapter 7

The journey continues

The next morning, after a cookies and chocolate breakfast, Daniel and Canica continue their journey.

"Let's explore this world," says the griffin. "Hop on my back and let's head somewhere else."

She didn't have to say it twice.

In the blink of an eye, they found themselves flying over the clouds.

The landscape began changing little by little, the candy forest was left behind and the first snow scraps started appearing.

"Daniel, look!" says Canica. "Down there!"

Daniel looks and a huge sense of joy washes over him.

"It's a village!" he says, seeing houses and buildings everywhere. "We'll find someone for sure!"

And again, Canica starts the descent maneuver.

Chapter 8

About the snow

Although it is snowing hard, Daniel isn't cold at all.

He strokes Canica's feathers and takes his hand back full of snow, but...

"It is sugar!" he assures after taking the tip of his tongue to the fake snow. "Powdered sugar!"

With no more comments, they start walking down the streets of the village.

Chapter 9

The village

It's deserted. There's no signs of life.

Daniel and Canica walk slowly, stepping over the stoned pathway quietly. On both sides of the street there's constructions. Mostly one story houses, modest homes made out of sugar.

To check he's right, Daniel heads towards a house and bites one of the bricks.

"As I expected, it's chocolate."

Then, he licks the fake marble steps that lead to the house's entrance.

"Mmmm," he says, thinking. "It's like... Like..." He lets the taste dance in his mouth. "Like... I got it, it's horchata flavored candy!"

Next, Daniel licks the door.

"This one is easy... It's a waffle!"

He is so focused with tasking the building materials that he doesn't hear the whispering behind him. Neither Daniel nor Canica realize the steps that, slowly, head towards them.

Daniel starts licking the house's glasses and Canica is focused on nibbling the snow that falls around her beak.

"Hey! You!" says a voice. "Hands up!"

Daniel, astonished, stops licking the window and with his hands on his head, he turns around slowly.

When he sees them, he almost faints.

Chapter 10
Our hero

They were not alone.

That world had inhabitants... Oh did it ever!

Like out of nowhere, hundreds of people have them surrounded. They form a big circle around them, blocking all exits.

"I-I-I d-d-d-idn't p-p-pret-t-tend to eat the house," Daniel apologizes. "I was only licking it a bit."

Canica runs towards Daniel and sticks by his side. She's also scared.

And not without reason.

The citizens of that wonderful world of sure are so weird, so fantastic, and as deliciously sugary as everything around them.

Daniel notices that the people, are actually, shaped like chocolate bars, sweets and candy.

There are dozens of giant donuts with two huge white gummies instead of eyes and long strawberry candies as legs. The boys and girls are shaped like spongy and bright gum caramels. There's all colors and flavors: orange boys, strawberry mince girls, cream sugar boys, sugary lemon girls...

And as if that wasn't enough, there's soft old men and soft old women of mince gum, all of them leaning in their caramel canes.

The giant donut, seems, it's the local policeman, just as his jelly marbled police hat gives away.

"We're just passing by," Canica apologizes. "We were just leaving... We don't want to bother anyone."

Slowly, Daniel and his friend start moving. They walk carefully, with no sudden moved, trying to make as little noise as possible.

But only after a few steps, the inhabitants start murmuring. They start with timid whispers, giving them furtive glances every now and then.

"What's happening?" Daniel asks Canica.

The griffin shrugs, without understanding.

The habitants start raising their voices... At first

they seemed fearful and scared but now... They seem happy.

As a matter of fact, one of the gummy children starts smiling.

"Are you sure?" asks a soft old lady to her soft husband. "Are you sure it's him?"

And, in a flash, all the neighbors were laughing, jumping and hugging each other.

"At last!" said a coconut popcorn mom. "He's here!"

"Gummies, chocolate bars and other members of Sugarville," said the policeman with a loud voice. "The day we have long awaited has arrived."

Daniel doesn't understand anything. What is all that supposed to be? Have they lost their minds?

"It's our hero!" yells someone.

"Our hero!" another voice repeats.

"Our hero!"

And everyone runs towards him. Everyone want to talk to Daniel, pet Canica, introduce themselves, give them presents, offer their houses for whenever they want to visit...

Chapter 11
More than welcome

When things calmed down, the Mayor of Sugarville went to pay his respects to Daniel and Canica.

"You are more than welcome!" he says shaking his hand and claw. "We have awaited your arrival for over a hundred years."

The Mayor is a long fried cookie filled with flan. While he was talking, Daniel's mouth was watering. Smells delicious! Actually, it has such an exquisite smell, that Daniel has to close his mouth to stop himself from drooling.

"Many in this village lost hope years ago," he explains, "but many more still hoped. We knew that, eventually, you would arrive."

They were at the Mayor's house, right next to the Town Hall.

Daniel sits down right across from the Mayor and Canica lays down on the floor, right next to him. The room in the Mayor's home is as spacious as it is delicious. A huge chocolate and vanilla swirl cookie table commands the room. The walls are made of checkered black and white chocolate cookies.

"Oh, by the way!" says the Mayor with his hand on his head. "My name is Juan! Excuse me, with the nerves, I had totally forgot to introduce myself."

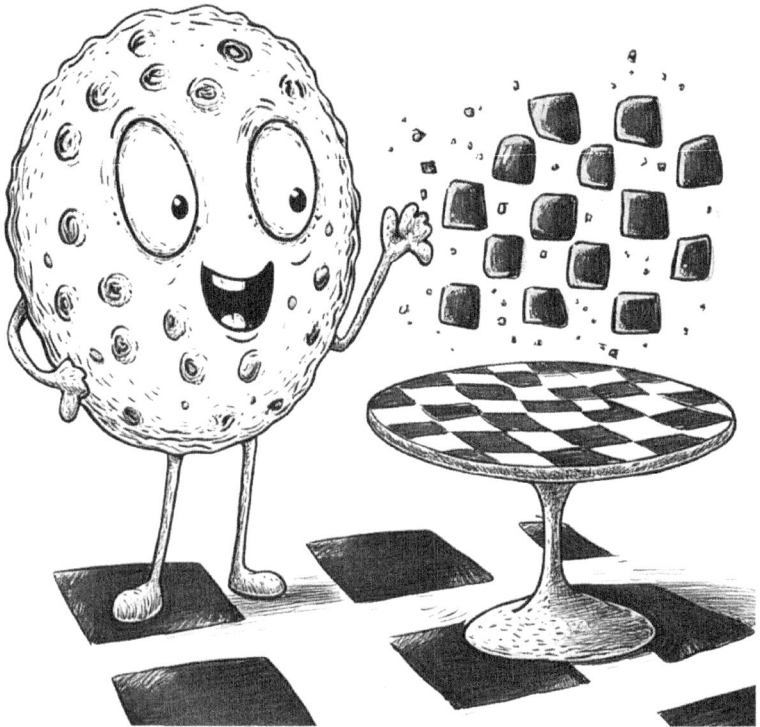

Daniel and Canica smile. Truth is, they feel right at home. The town's hospitality is extraordinary.

"Juan," says Daniel, staring at him. "What happened? Where are we? Why is everything made out of sugar in here?"

The Mayor sights, shaking his head heavily.

"It would be better if we take a walk."

Chapter 12
Who is Valentine?

They start walking down a path downtown. There's shoe stores, a hairdressers, a library and... Even a school!

Mayor Juan walks in the middle, with Daniel to his right and Canica to his left. Everyone, and although they have already introduced themselves, wave at them when they see them, always smiling.

"In the past, everything was normal," says the Mayor, nodding at a passerby. "As you can imagine, I wasn't born being a fried cookie, nor were any of the things you see here originally made out of sugar."

The Mayor stops. It seems like even talking about it is hard for him, as if the mere fact of remembering it gives him great pain.

"Before I was a fried cookie, I was a man. I had brown hair, brown skin and blue eyes. I was a person like any other Daniel, like you."

"And what happened?" asks Daniel, unable to contain himself. "How is it possible that everything changed so much?"

The Mayor shuts his eyes, stopping.

"The one to blame is Valentine," he whispers.

Canica and Daniel exchange a surprised look.

"And who is Valentine?"

"Don't say his name loud," he corrects him, looking around to make sure no one heard. "People in this village freak out just by hearing his name..."

They kept on walking. The Mayor led them to a nice park where some bushy apple licorices gave a fresh shade. They sat down in one of the benches.

"Valentine is a wizard," he explained. "Don't get me wrong, I don't mean to say that all wizards are bad. In this world, there have been magicians that have done a lot of good things for everyone. But Valentine used all his power to do evil."

Daniel and Canica stayed respectfully silent, waiting for Juan to carry on:

"You see... There's something I have to tell you," the Mayor clicked his tongue. "In this town, we've always kind of had a sweet tooth."

"Sweet tooth?"

"Yes, yes.... I mean, we've always liked eating candy. I myself, ate a chocolate bar every day."

"I like chocolate too!" said Daniel, smiling.

The Mayor look at him darkly.

"The thing, Daniel and Canica, is that a bad day Valentine heard of our fondness for candy, and that evil wizard thought it would be fun to turn us all into candy and goods."

The Mayor sunk his feet in the park grass, which actually was thin strips of spicy mint.

"In the beginning, we went crazy," he continues to explain. "The first days we were ecstatic, going from here to there, eating everything we found. And everything was delicious. At first we weren't very concerned about our new looks... We actually thought it was funny. We all thought it was a game from Valentine, that he was pranking us for April Fool's Day and that he would soon return us to our original form. But..."

Juan's voice began to tremble.

"But weeks went by and everything remained the same. People began to worry. No one wanted to taste sugar anymore. We were all sick of the damn chocolate. We just wanted to get back our lives, to go back to normal."

"Did you talk to Valentine?" intervened Canica. "Did you tell him his joke was no longer funny?"

"I talked to him myself, but he wouldn't budge," says the mayor, his face darkening. "He would only laugh. He said no. That he would never break the spell."

"But that's not fair!" exclaims Daniel. "It is one thing is that you like eating candy and it is a whole different thing for you to spend your lives turned into candy."

"There has to be a way to break the spell!" says Canica, snapping her tail like a whip. "This can't go on any longer! It's crazy!"

"You're right Canica," says the Mayor. "It's absolutely crazy."

And with no warning, he starts to cry. Candy tears start streaming from his eyes in a colorful cascade.

"You can't imagine what it's like to live like this," Juan sinks his face in Canica's feathers. "In this town everyone hates sugar. Having candy for breakfast, lunch, snacks and diner is torture. We all have rotten teeth." And to match his words, Juan shows them his teeth. He barely has a couple of them, yellow and decaying.

"Since Valentine cursed us, we have tried leading a normal life," Juan says, regaining his composure and pulling his head out of the griffin's feathers. "People still go to their jobs and kids go to school, but to be honest, it is torture. In summer we melt and the worst is we can't even bathe at the beach, because the water... Water doesn't exist anymore. The entire sea is chocolate!"

Daniel nods in silence, remembering the river of liquid chocolate that he found in the woods.

"The chocolate sea is extremely dangerous because it is so thick, that it swallows anyone that dares step in it."

"It must be terrible living like that!" Canica and Daniel have barely been there a day and they are already starting to hate sugar. They can't even imagine what the inhabitants of the village must have gone through.

"We have tried everything we can think of to get rid of the sugar," explains Juan. "We searched for fruit and vegetable seeds and cultivated them but... Everything that springs from this earth is coated with sugar!"

Juan looks up at the sky, without hope.

"I would give up my cookie legs just to try lettuce again... Fresh lettuce, well diced, seasoned with oil and vinegar..."

Juan had to hold back. Just the thought of such treat drove him out of his mind.

"We will go talk to Valentine!" Daniel said, standing. "We will put an end to this madness!"

The Mayor, despite his anguish, smiles.

"Would you really do that?" his eyes sparkle. "We would be eternally grateful!"

Chapter 13
The mission

The entire village gathered in the plaza. Daniel and Canica were going to talk to Valentine and they all wanted to show their support.

"Be very careful!" a lollipop man said. "Valentine is as powerful as he is dangerous!"

"Here!" said a cotton candy, giving them a basket. "For the road, just in case you get hungry."

Daniel hadn't thought of that. In that world, everything was sugar, everything was food. If they were hungry, they could stop anywhere and eat anything. They didn't need to carry any food.

However, Daniel was polite and took the basket from the woman. Inside, there were several chocolate bottles to quench their thirst and tons of donuts and bagels to eat.

"Thank you very much lady!" he said, strapping the basket to Canica's reins.

Canica was prepared for the occasion. The made her, with delicious golden sugar thread, a riding chair similar to a horse's, but way bigger. Because Canica was huge.

They needed four candies to strap it to her back, but once set, it looked spectacular.

"You look so pretty!" says Daniel, hoping on.

"I know!" she says, smugly.

The chair is incredibly comfortable. Besides, it has a ton of pockets to put stuff in.

"All our blessings go to you!" the Mayor says, stroking Canica just below her beak. "Daniel, Canica... You're our last hope."

Daniel swallows, feeling the enormous responsibility that adventure means.

"It's a long road," he explains. "Remember you have to go always north"

All the citizens nod, like they all knew exactly where Valentine lives.

"On the fifth day, you will find a huge mountain. You will recognize it when you see it, because it's the biggest there is."

Canica extends her front legs, stretching elegantly. The road is going to be long, very long... Perhaps, too long.

"That mountain is where Valentine lives," the Mayor concludes. "Be very careful... I don't think he'll be very friendly."

"Don't worry," Daniel says, holding tight to the

reins. He's not sure why, but he thinks it'll be a bumpy road. "We will take care of Valentine. Canica and me will talk to him and show him the right path."

And then, Canica starts gathering speed.

The villagers make a hallway and say goodbye to their heroes throwing candy rose petals at them.

"You're the best!"

"Come back soon!"

"We love you!"

"Hail our heroes!"

Canica gathers more speed. The entire world becomes blurry around them. Daniel sees the thousands of faces of the people gathered on both sides of the improvised flight track. He know their future is now in his hands.

Daniel purses his lips, so they look like a straight line.

"Let's go Canica! Fly!"

The griffin extends her mighty wings

BOOOMMMMM – BOOOMMMMM-
BOOOMMMMMMM

She starts flapping.

BOOMM- BOMMM- BOOMM- BOOMM-
BOOMM- BOOMM

Faster, faster, faster...

BOOMM, BOOMM, BOOMM, BOOMM,
BOOMM

They take off.

Daniel lets go of the reins. He feels safe, like Canica and he are a single being.

With crushing confidence, Daniel raises his hands and starts waving, saying goodbye to all those wonderful people.

The cheering, the applause, the rolling tears... It all falls behind as Canica gets higher.

After a few minutes, they are flying over a sea of clouds.

Chapter 14

Trust me

The road was long, very long... Perhaps, too long.

Although they were flying at all speed on Canica's back, they took longer that they should have. They got lost several times. They had to turn around and retrace their steps. They had to stop and look for food. They had to look for a safe place to spend the night. But mostly, they had to gather their bearings.

"Are you sure that north is this way?" Daniel asks.

Even though the Mayor said that in five days they would find their destination, there was no trace of the mountain where Valentine lives.

They have been flying over that wonderful sugar world for over two weeks and still haven't found anything.

"We're lost!" Daniel wants to find Valentine once and for all, wants to talk to him, convince him to break the spell and above all, wants to go back home.

They have been eating candy, chocolate and gummies since they arrived and, to be honest, he's sick of them. Even though he tries not to eat a lot, his belly hurts because of all the sugar.

He had never missed a taste of French omelet, a carrot or a good plate of lentils so badly...

"Trust me, Daniel!" Canica is so relaxed. "We're headed in the right direction, trust me. It's just a matter of time before we reach..."

The mountain!

It shows up out of nowhere, with no warning. The mere sight is impressive.

It's huge. Juan was right: they would recognize it by just looking at it.

The mountain is different from all the others. The first thing that sets it apart is its size: colossal, immense... So talk that it rises above the clouds, like it has no end.

The second thing that makes the mountain unique is its color: it's not a colorful gummy mountain. No. This mountain is made of solidified honey, which makes it a spectacular shade of gold.

Daniel has to squint, blinded by its shine.

"What did I tell you?" Canica extends her wings and lets herself be drafted by the warm air currents. "I told you we were going in the right direction!"

Daniel and his friend watch Valentine's home fascinated. It takes them more than ten minutes to fly around it...

"Where is the entrance?" Daniel asks, looking up and down looking for a door or something similar.

Canica flaps her wings hard and they start ascending.

"Maybe Valentine lives at the top," says Canica tentatively.

But as much as Canica flaps her wings, as high as they fly, they don't come close to seeing the top. The mountain continues going up without stop, like it was a living being that continues to grow.

"This is not a normal mountain!" Daniel concludes. "Valentine has to have bewitched it..."

They fly high, very high. Canica looks down and the entire world seems to have vanished. There is no trace of the Candy Woods, no trace of the huge hot cocoa sea that had always accompanied them.

The only thing that seems to go up and down is the huge cylinder of solid honey that seems to grow and grow.

And, as Canica flies higher and higher, they start to run out of oxygen. It's getting harder to breathe.

"We better descend," the griffin says. "It's too dangerous."

Canica hollows out her wings but, instead of losing altitude, a powerful current wraps around them, dragging them upwards.

Daniel hangs on with all his strength to Canica's reins. They both start screaming:

"Noooooooooooooooo!"

It's out of their hands.

They keep going up at all speed, like blown by a hurricane. They rolled and rolled. Canica lost her flight position and... Ends up upside down and with her head down, staring at the void, which gets bigger every second.

Daniel is about to gall, but he hangs on to

Canica's neck and manages to stick to her.

They keep gaining altitude and...

The wind stops.

They're not at the top of the honey mountain, which keeps extending to the stars, but the found an opening.

"An entrance!" Daniel can barely believe it. "Canica, is the entrance!"

The griffin flaps her right wing, manages to get right side up and without hesitating, head towards it at all speed.

That adventure almost cost them their lives. They are very nervous, so much that they don't realize that, from inside the entrance, wrapped in darkness, a pair of eyes are watching them.

Chapter 15

The only light

The inside of the mountain is fresh. Not even close to the hot outside.

Daniel dismounts Canica and starts walking.

The thread carefully. Their steps resound, revealing their presence.

It's dark. They barely see where they are stepping.

Daniel swallows, feeling his heartbeat smash against his chest.

He knows they shouldn't be there. He knows this is Valentine's house and no one invited them in.

"Do you think valentine will be angry?" You can tell by her voice that Canica is afraid. She's almost as scared as Daniel.

"I don't know."

A light shines. It's orange and it glares in the dark.

"It's there," Daniel whispers. "Valentine is

there..."

They hold their breath and with trembling steps, they approach.

The light grows bigger. Daniel and Canica discover a wide room. The walls are golden and the roof... There is no roof. Or at least, if there is, they can't see it.

There's a bunch of chocolate coins and lying on top of them, is Valentine.

He's not asleep.

"I was waiting for you!" he says, smiling.

Chapter 16
A minor detail

There's something no one told them about Valentine. A detail that neither the Mayor of Sugarville nor any of the inhabitants told them: Valentine is a dragon.

The evil wizard, besides being immensely powerful, is a DRAGON.

"A-a-aaar-re you Valentine?" Daniel stutters.

Valentine leans his head towards Daniel's. It is so much bigger than Canica's that, as a matter of fact, the griffin looks like a little bird next to him.

"Yes Daniel, my name is Valentine," he has a deep voice and the entre ground shakes.

As it happens with dogs, fish and birds, there a lot of different kinds of dragons. Valentine is a magical dragon and, as all members of his species, can't spit fire. On the contrary, in his insides is a powerful magic.

"How do you know my name?" asks Daniel, trying to steady himself.

Valentine arches his huge mouth. He has sharp teeth.

"Daniel," he says, tasting every word. "I can read your mind."

Daniel steadies himself and tries not to think about anything. He tries to keep his mind blank.

If Valentine can read his mind, he surely saw how scared he is.

Canica hits Daniel, as if the presence of her friend comforts her.

"Hi Canica!" says Valentine. "How are you, little bird?"

"I'm a griffin!" she corrects him, in an act of valor. "Can't you see my lion body?"

Valentine seems to find that amusing.

"Of course, of course," he says, smiling even wider. "Whatever you say little bird."

Valentine is colossal, but for a dragon, he's not that big. That's because magical dragons are not especially famous for their size.

Valentine has red skin, with yellow and green stripes. His head is long, like a snake's and instead of horns, two large antennae balance behind his ears.

"We've come here so you put an end to the curse," says Daniel, cutting straight to the chase.

Valentine starts laughing. Daniel smells his breath that, to his surprise, is minty fresh.

"It's not funny!" says Daniel.

Even though he is shaking, he tries to look tough, sure of himself.

"The inhabitants of Sugarville are sick of your spell!" he explains, pissed off. "They can't keep living like this."

Chapter 17
Deal?

Daniel and Canica explained to Valentine all the motives why he should break the spell:

The explained that many of them had rotten teeth, that they had belly aches, that they were sick of eating so much sugar, that they melted in the summer from the heat, that they couldn't bathe at the beach because the water was actually thick chocolate...

Canica even explained how in Sugarville, they had tried cultivating fruit, vegetables and other greens, but it was all in vain.

When they are done talking, Valentine says nothing. He hasn't stopped smiling for an instant... And the truth is, his smile doesn't inspire a lot of confidence.

"Summarizing," says Valentine, burying his wings in the coins. "You come to my house and demand that I undo my spell. Is that right?"

Daniel and Canica look at each other and nod. "That's it!"

"And tell me..." Valentine stretches his neck and approaches his head until it is right in front of them. "What if I don't want to? Huh? Are you going to make me?"

Valentine is having a great time.

Canica hides her tail between her legs, scared.

"Ah... Of course!" Valentine smiles even wider and it makes them more nervous. The wider he smiles, the more teeth you can see... And they are very big.

"Please, Valentine," begs Daniel. "Give them back their lives... Make the sugar go away."

The dragon turns his head sideways.

"I have a question, Daniel," he says, licking his snout with his tongue. "And what if instead of undoing my spell, I turn you into candy? Don't you think that would be fun?"

Valentine smiles a bit more, and in doing so, his smiles transforms. It's no longer friendly, it is cruel.

Daniel hugs Canica. Before Valentine, they feel more insignificant than ever.

"No... Please," says Canica, holding back the tears. "Don't do that..."

And just when she's about to cry, Valentine starts laughing.

Daniel and Canica look at each other, lost at words.

"I'm teasing you!" the magician says. "It was a joke!"

Daniel strokes Canica under her beak, which relaxes her.

"Look, I'll make you a deal." Valentine abandons the comfort of his chocolate coins bed and stands. He stretches, extending his wings. "Do you like riddles?"

Daniel and Canica, confused by the question, nod.

"Yes, yes... I love riddles!" Daniel starts relaxing.

"Well then," Valentine combs his head's antennae with his claws. "We'll make a game: you two against me. Each one will come up with three riddles... If you guys win, I promise I will break the spell."

"And what if we lose?" inquires Canica.

"In that case..." Valentine gives them that snake smile again. "I will turn you into candy and you will be my servants. This mountain could use a good clean up!"

Canica and Daniel are shocked. That deal is crazy but...

"We accept!" Daniel extends his hand.

Valentine extends his claw and shakes his hand with the tip of his little finger's nail.

"Deal!"

Chapter 18

Let the show begin!

Valentine goes to one end of the room and Daniel and Canica to the opposite.

"We have to win!" Daniel whispers to his griffin. "I don't know about you, but I don't feel like staying here my whole life, sweeping this mountain and serving Valentine breakfast.

Canica shuts his eyes, agreeing with him.

"We have to think up three riddles," points out Daniel. "Do you know any?"

Canica shrugs her shoulders.

"Nothing," she says. "I don't know any..."

Even at the distance, they hear Valentine's whispering. He is getting ready for the riddle contest...

"Well in that case, let me speak. I know three really difficult riddles!"

Daniel hops on Canica's back and in two flaps they fly over to the center of the room.

"We're ready!" they let him know. "Should we start?"

Chapter 19

Three points

Valentine clarified the rules of the competition.

"Whoever scores three points, wins," he repeated. "Whoever gets the riddle right, scores a point. If the riddle isn't guessed right, the point goes to the one proposing the riddle. In case of a tie, and extra riddle round will be done and so on until we determine the winner. Ready?"

Daniel is very sure of himself. Besides, on Canica's back, he is more comfortable and can think better.

"Alright then," Valentine lies on the ground. "As you are my guests, you start."

A big silence follows, broken only by the crackle of the torches that illuminate the room.

Daniel swallows and asks the first riddle:

"I have a head and a tail but no body. What am I?"

Valentine is petrified.

"A tail and a head but no body..." the dragon repeats. "What is it? What is it?"

Like it helps him think, Valentine laps around the room.

"What is it? A head... A tail... No body... I got it!"

Valentine runs until he's in front of Daniel and Canica.

"I know! What has a tail and a head but no body is a snake."

"Wrong!" Valentine grabs his head with his claws. "It's a coin"

"A coin...." Valentine can't believe it. He just lost. The kid and the griffin are winning 1-0. "Now it is my turn" Valentine smiles. "I won't make it easy!"

Daniel stares, defying.

"What gets wetter and wetter the more it dries? What is is?"

And Valentine, satisfied with his riddle, starts laughing. He knows they will never find the answer. Never...

"A towel!" answers Daniel.

Valentine pulls his antennae. He is clearly nervous. He's losing 2-0.

"It's our turn" Daniel poses his next riddle. "What is at the end of a rainbow?"

Valentine ponders:

"At the end of the rainbow... I know! A pot of gold!"

The dragon answers:

"A pot of gold."

Daniel laughs.

"Wrong again!"

"It's not possible! It's not possibleeeee!"

"It's the letter W!"

Valentine starts screaming.

"You're cheaters! You're damn cheaters!"

"We won fair and square," says Canica. "You lost 3-0. Now stay true to your word. Undo the spell."

The dragon, rabid, serpentines until he reaches Daniel. The kid is mounted on his griffin and looks triumphant, with the satisfaction that only riddle contests winners have.

"There is something I haven't told you," Valentine confesses. "I'm a liar! And now, I will turn ou into candy."

Valentine's eyes start changing color. They become blue... And brighter...

"Run!" Canica turns around and starts running to the mountain's entrance. "Faster, faster, faster!"

When Valentine releases his spell, Daniel and Canica are already out of sight.

"Damn intruders!"

This will not end like this.

Valentine starts running after them.

Chapter 20
Into the void

Valentine runs towards the exit, and with a jump, throws himself into the void. He falls at all speed, right behind the spot already disappearing into the abyss.

Daniel and Canica try to escape. The griffin is fast, but Valentine is a magical dragon.

He extends his wings and lets the wind give him impulse. He is fast. Each time faster.

He approaches.

Chapter 21
An idea

Run, Canica!" Daniel can barely hear his own voice. The sound of the air crashing against his face is deafening.

Canica turns her head, and what she sees, almost paralyze her.

Valentine is right behind them. He's rocketing down the mountain, chasing them.

You can tell he is furious. And that they managed to escape just in time.

"He's getting closer!" Daniel is terrified. The huge mass of scales and wings is right on their heels.

"I can't go any faster!" Canica protests.

They have already descended a lot. At this moment, they are going through clouds and under their feet they start seen the tops of trees. To his left is the chocolate ocean. It extends towards the horizon, covering everything in a delicious almond color.

Canica folds her wings more, trying to gain speed, but Valentine is also coming in close, relentless.

"He's going to catch us!"

They are terrified, If Valentine manages to capture them, they will spend the rest of their lives turned into candy wiping and polishing his infinite honey mountain...

"He's getting closer!" Canica yells. "He's on top of us!"

Daniel turns. It's true. He's on them... Barely a few inches away. They can almost smell her breath.

"I have an idea!"

Chapter 22

The chocolate sea

Canica turns and heads towards the chocolate sea.

"Are you sure Daniel?"

But there is no time for questions. There is no time to think, just to react.

The chocolate sea is dangerous. They know that very well. Mayor Juan warned him when he said that, despite the summer heat, no one would think of taking a bath in the sea. And that's because the chocolate is extremely thick...

And yet, Canica and Daniel are headed over there at all speed.

Its surface was calm. No waves, just a soft bubbling. Actually, that sea has to have very hot chocolate, because steam was rising out of it, flooding everything with a sweet mist.

"We're going to burn!"

"Keep going straight!" Daniel commands. "Trust me. Wait for my sign!"

The keep going down. They are free falling. Valentine can almost bite Canica's tail... His shadow projects over the chocolate surface, darkening it suddenly. Canica and Daniel go through the mist and see the bubbling chocolate.

They are about to crash in...

"NOOOOOW!"

Canica leans upwards and flaps her wings with all her strength. He curves up and starts flying over the surface. Her paws scratch the chocolate. It's burning and you can tell it is very thick.

But Valentine doesn't have time to maneuver.

In comparison with the griffin, the dragon is a giant. He is so focused in biting Canica's rail, he doesn't realize that he is about to crash.

When Valentine looks up, it's already too late.

The chocolate sea is right in front of him. Very close. So close that, in spite of spreading his huge wings, he can't do anything to correct his course.

Besides, he is very heavy. To rise up, he needs more space.

Unable to do anything, Valentine crashes.

Chapter 23

Help!

The crash is deafening. The chocolate flies everywhere. Valentine roars in pain.

"Heeeeelp!" he screams "I can't swim!"

The wizard moves his wings, in a desperate attempt to get out of the chocolate, but he only manages to sink in further.

The chocolate sea waters act like quick sand.

It starts swallowing him.

Valentine stretches his neck, but keeps on sinking. He can barely breathe. He's about to vanish...

"We have to do something!" says Daniel. "He's going to die!"

Canica circles around the dragon. You can no longer see his long pointy tail or his wings... Even his antennae start disappearing.

"Head for the shore!" commands Daniel. "Quick!"

Chapter 24

It's too dangerous

Valentine's scream get lost behind them. Canica lands on the shore and Daniel hops off at once. He runs to a tree and starts stripping away the bark. The trunk is hard licorice. I's well coiled and looks pretty resistant.

Daniel pulls and pulls, until he has a large pile of licorice rope at his feet.

He hands an end to Canica, who grabs it with his beak and Daniel knots the other end to his ankle.

"Let's save that dragon!"

Canica, without losing a second, takes off. She holds the licorice rope highly and pulls Daniel, who shoots through the air.

Daniel, hanging upside down, flies over the chocolate see several feet below Canica. Under his feet he can see his friend's pink underbelly and under his head, the bubbling chocolate sea.

He starts looking for Valentine, but there's no

trace of him.

"Valentiiiiine!" he calls, using his hands to make a speaker. "Valentiiiiineeee!"

But he hears nothing. Canica flies over the sea... Is too big and she doesn't know the exact place where they last saw the dragon.

Maybe it's too late. Maybe they took too long and Valentine has drowned...

"Hey!" signals Canica. "Over there!"

The only thing left of Valentine is a shadow sinking beneath the surface of the sea. It's fading, disappearing, sinking.

"I'm going to grab him!" says Daniel.

"What are you saying?" yells Canica from above. "It's too dangerous!"

"I have the rope," Daniel reminds her. "I'll look for him, grab him and you pull up, got it?"

There was no time to argue.

Daniel's plan was crazy, but it was the only one they had. Begrudgingly, Canica yields, and starts descending.

Daniel dives into the thick chocolate.

Chapter 25
Ask Daniel

Diving in chocolate is nothing like diving in water. If you doubt it, ask Daniel.

When Daniel submerges, everything becomes brown. He wades down, towards the huge shadow that is little by little, sinking, getting lost in the depths.

He has a hard time moving because the chocolate is so dense. Rather than liquid, it is like some sort of fine mass.

But Daniel doesn't give up and he does his best to keep swimming downwards. Now he can see Valentine: the dragon has his wings extended, his tail coiled up and the long neck extended looking towards the surface...

Daniel doesn't know if he is dead. Maybe it's too late. Valentine might have been an evil wizard, but he didn't deserve to die. No one does.

Daniel, stroke by stroke, approaches his head. It's all brown, visibility is very bad. He stares in his eyes, with the hope of finding in them a tell-tale glimmer of life. But they are closed...

Daniel grabs hold of the magical dragon's antennae and gives the rope attached to his foot, two thugs.

It's the signal.

Chapter 26

Two thugs

Canica flies over the site of the accident in small circles. There's no sight of Daniel. Canica bites hard the rope in her beak. She won't let go for anything in the world.

She knows her friend's life depends on that rope. If she dropped it, he would never come out of the Chocolate Sea's waters.

Every second, Canica gets more and more nervous.

She descends and glides closer to the surface, but you can't see anything down there. Just the bubbling of the hot cocoa...

Two thugs.

Two thugs!

It's the signal.

Canica flies up but she can't move. She flaps and flaps her wings like a small bird unable to take flight.

Down there, Daniel must have grab hold of

Valentine. And Valentine is very heavy. Even if magical dragons are not very heavy, they can easily weight as much as ten cows.

And Canica is not very big. She can fly, true, and can carry a little extra weight, but that is too much.

She flaps and flaps, moves and moves her wings, but she barely moves.

And that's when she thinks of Daniel...

He's been in there too long! He's not going to be able to hold his breath much longer!

Canica, with no idea of how she's doing it, pulls and pulls. Her beak hurts but she won't let go of the rope. He pulls up again. And again. And harder...

Chapter 27

Fresh air

Daniel breathes again. The fresh air floods his lungs. He feels reborn.

Valentine has also pulled his head out. He is alive. He still breathes.

The dragon looks at the kid and then at the griffin flying just above their heads.

Canica drags them to the shore.

Finally, they step on dry land.

Chapter 28

Up to their nose

Daniel and Valentine spit hot cocoa out their mouths. The liquid got even up their noses. They were just about to drown.

Canica descends and lies under the fresh shadow of a tree. She's exhausted, she needs to rest.

Daniel sits on the floor and watches the dragon. Valentine has extended his wings on the sand and is drying off. Surely with that much chocolate stuck to them, he can't move.

"Why?" he asks. "Why have you done it?"

"Done what?" asks Daniel, panting.

"Why did you have me?" Valentine moves his tail, uncurls it and extends it over the caramel sand. "I've tried to turn you into candy and you still risked your lives to save me... Why?"

"Because it's what anyone would have done," Canica answers.

And Valentine's face starts changing. It doesn't

look so much like a snake's... His eyes start watering and somehow, Daniel and Canica start sensing his sadness.

"I've been very bad," Valentine says, letting the tears roll down his scaly skin. "Those people didn't deserve what I did to them... You guys didn't deserve the way I treated you... I'm a monster..."

And Valentine starts crying bitterly. A cascade of tears slides down his cheeks. The dragon lets his head drop on the sand, feeling the weight of his own shame.

"I am the worst wizard in the world!" he yells.

Canica and Daniel stand up and start petting him. At first, Valentine is scared, but he quickly gives in and lets them scratch behind his ears, between his eyes and under his chin.

He relaxes. He feels so much better.

"You can still undo this," whispers Daniel, patting his antennae.

Valentine looks at him in respectful silence.

"Yes, Mister Dragon," Canica says. "Just break your spell... Let this world go back to what it was...

Let the people regain their old bodies! Everyone will thank you!"

"No! No! No! A thousand times no!" Valentine starts crying again. "They will never forgive me! For them I will always be the wizard that turned everything into sugar... They will always remember me as a monster."

"You're not a monster," Daniel pets him, making small circles on his cheek. "Besides, I think everyone has learned a valuable lesson with your spell."

"You really think so?" Valentine says, looking at him, hopeful.

Daniel and Canica nod.

"Before, they all had a sweet tooth," Canica explains. "Mayor Juan told us. He told us they ate a lot of chocolate, candy, sugar. But now... They all want to eat fruits and vegetables!"

The dragon raises his head. Knowing that, despite his evil spell, he had accomplished something good was unknown to him.

"Actually, they have tried cultivating fruits and

vegetables" Daniel continues. "They are dreaming of eating lettuce and delicious vegetables!"

Valentine leans on his forearms and with a lot of effort, manages to stand up. He still has a lot of chocolate sticking to his scales, but he is starting to dry up.

"So, they won't hate me?"

"Not at all!" Canica assures him. "You have taught them a valuable lesson that they will thank for the rest of their lives: the importance of having a healthy, balanced diet.

Valentine lifts his wings, snaps them and lets the pieces of solid chocolate fall off.

"Alright..."

Chapter 29

The blue ray

In Sugarville, something extraordinary is happening.

The gum children go out to the school yard so they can see it with their own eyes, the clerks are leaving their stores, the farmers stop their work and even Mayor Juan leaves his office at the Town Hall and goes out into the street to watch the commotion.

"What's happening?" he asks a toast that runs nearby

"He did it!" she says euphoric. "He did it!"

Juan raises his sight.

"No way" he says astounded. "It's impossible..."

A huge blue ray rises in the distance, up into the sky.

I've seen that ray... Once, many years ago...

"Valentine." Juan starts running with all his neighbors. "Valentine, Valentine!"

They all cheer his name.

"Valentine! Valentine! Valentine!"

The blue ray is getting bigger, higher, brighter, and more magical.

"Valentine, Valentine, Valentine!"

The ray explodes, expanding its light all over the world. As it passes, the sugar disappears. The trees go back to being just trees, the animals recover their original bodies, and the chocolate sea turns back into wonderful salt water and the people...

Juan watches his hands, his fingers, his nails... he touches his face, his cheeks, his moustache...

The people hug each other. The children have stopped being gummies, the giant waffles with arms and legs have disappeared and so have the chatty brittle cookies...

"Herminia! It's you!"

Juan hugs his neighbor. The woman dissolves in tears.

At the school, they open the doors and children and teachers run out. They all run towards the orchard. There, the farmers pick up the tomatoes that, for the first time in forever, are not made of sugar.

The kids eat the tomatoes and when they chew, they can barely believe it.

"They're delicious!"

Juan and his neighbor go to an apple tree and grab a bunch of apples. They bite them, they chew them and they let that delicious flavor dance in their palates.

After a few hours, the neighbors gather in the town plaza. They all have bags filled with lettuces, carrots, pears and other fruits, vegetables and greens.

Juan climbs up the steps and, asking for silence, rises his apple like a toast.

"To Daniel and Canica!"

The neighbors raise their fruits.

"To Daniel and Canica!" they repeat in unison.

Next, they all take a loud bite out of their fruits.

That boy and his good friend Canica did it. They can't even imagine the long road they had to travel to reach Valentine's home. They can't imagine how difficult it must have been for them to convince the evil dragon to break his crazy spell...

Daniel and Canica. They will never forget their names. Never.

In the town plaza, people start getting excited, the talking increases to shouts of joy.

"It's them!" says a little girl, pointing with her finger to the sky. "Our heroes!"

Two dots approach at maximum speed: one is small and the other one is huge.

"What are they?" a kid asks his teacher. "What is that?

But the teacher doesn't answer. They all raise their eyes and watch as those dots grow bigger and bigger. Several seconds pass until, finally, Juan recognizes them:

"It's Canica!" he says, pointing with his finger. "And that one over there must be... Valentine."

It is as a matter of fact, a dragon. Next to him, the griffin looks like a simple bird but...

"Where is Daniel?"

The kid is not on his griffin's back. Actually, you can see the mount they gave him completely empty.

"There he is!"

And they all see him.

Daniel is riding on Valentine's back, holding on to his antennae with his left hand and waving at everyone with his right.

The plaza bursts in applause and cheers.

Chapter 30

You're late

"Daniel" a voice calls him. "Daniel!"

Daniel turns in his bed, He's very sleepy

"You're going to be late for school!"

Daniel gets startled.

"Where am I?" he asks his mother.

His mother puts up the rooms curtains, letting the morning rays illuminate all the walls. Canica, his faithful friend, is back to being a dog. The Chihuahua runs around his mother's feet, her tiny tail wagging excitedly.

"Where are you?" his mother says smiling. "You're home! Where would you be?"

"Then, there is fruit?"

His mother is still astounded.

"Of course yes! Fruits, vegetables, eggs, meat... There's everything."

Daniel gets up and hugs his mom. It seems like forever since he last hugged her.

"I love you very much mommy!" he says.

"You're being weird Daniel. Are you ok?"

Daniel nods.

"Today after school, can I have some lentils?"

His mother is shocked. She puts a hand to his forehead.

"Do you have a fever Daniel? Are you feeling alright?"

Daniel smiles.

"I've never been better."

Your Review and Word-of-Mouth Recommendations Will Make a Difference

Reviews and word-of-mouth recommendations are crucial for any author to succeed. If you enjoyed this book, please leave a review, even if it is only a line or two, and tell your friends about it. It will help the author bring you new books and allow others to also enjoy the book.

Your support is greatly appreciated!

Discover more books by A.P. Hernandez:

www.aphernandez.com

I DON'T WANT TO READ!

A.P. Hernández

I DON'T WANT TO GO TO SCHOOL!

A.P. Hernández

I DON'T WANT TO RECYCLE!

A.P. Hernández

I DON'T WANT TO EXERCISE!

A.P. Hernández

I DON'T WANT TO BRUSH MY TEETH!

A.P. Hernández

JAIME AND THE REALM OF FANTASY

A.P. Hernández

PIRATE ACADEMY

A.P. Hernández

THE PUPPY PIANIST

A.P. Hernández

MARCUS SUPER PENGUIN TO THE RESCUE!

A.P. Hernández

VALERIE AND THE FAIRY KINGDOM
DODONA I FAIRY TALE

A.P. Hernández

A BLACK CAT'S LUCK

A.P. Hernández

I WANT IT NOW!

A.P. Hernández

THE WONDERFUL WORLD CHOCOLATE

A.P. Hernández

ADVENTURES AT THE BOTTOM OF THE SEA
IN SEARCH OF THE RED FISH

A.P. Hernández

RAUL A VERY POLAR BEAR

A.P. Hernández

A HALLOWEEN STORY

A.P. Hernández

Printed in Great Britain
by Amazon